THE BEST OF THE BARGAIN

adapted from a Polish folktale

BY JANINA DOMANSKA

GREENWILLOW BOOKS

A DIVISION OF WILLIAM MORROW & COMPANY, INC., NEW YORK

Copyright © 1977 by Janina Domanska. All rights reserved. No part of this book may be reproduced or utilized in any form or by any means electronic or mechanical, including photocopying, recording or by any information storage and retrieval system, without permission in writing from the Publisher. Inquiries should be addressed to Greenwillow Books, 105 Madison Ave., New York, N.Y. 10016. Printed in the United States of America.
1   2   3   4   5   6   7   8   9   10

Library of Congress Cataloging in Publication Data
Domanska, Janina. The best of the bargain   Summary: A hedgehog outsmarts a fox when they decide to share their land and crops. [1. Folklore — Poland] I. Title.
PZ8.1.D717Ku   398.2′452   76-13010   ISBN 0-688-80062-9
ISBN 0-688-84062-0 lib. bdg.

To Marysia and Witek

Olek the fox owned the apple orchard.
Hugo the hedgehog owned the field.
Olek said to Hugo, "If we can work your field
together and share the crop between us,
I'll give you half the fruit from my orchard."

"Very well," said Hugo,
"but let us settle one thing first.
  Which half will you take — the half that grows
  above the ground or the half that grows below the ground?"
"I would like the upper half," Olek replied.
"We will plant potatoes," decided Hugo.

They plowed the field.

They planted the potatoes.

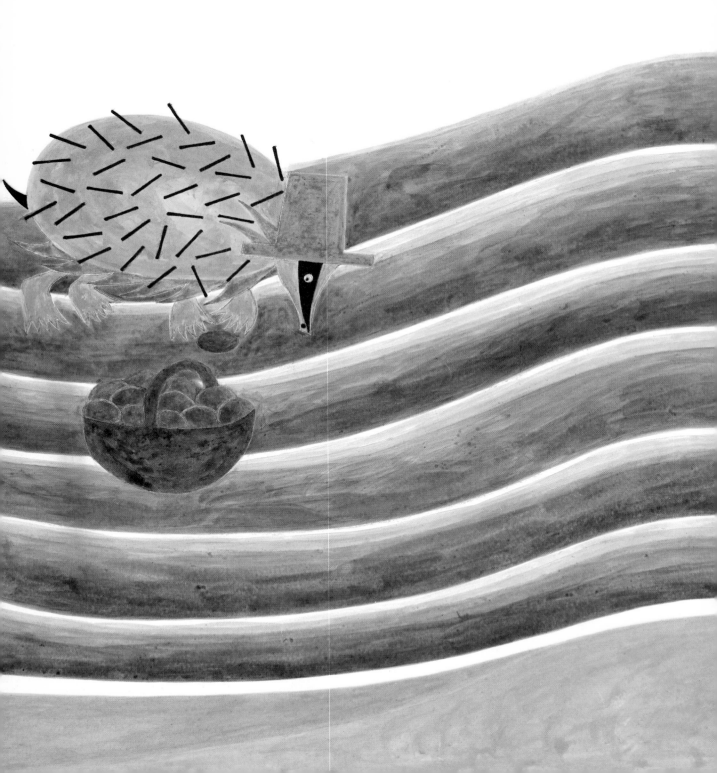

The potatoes grew. When harvesttime came,
Hugo said to Olek, "What grows above the ground
is yours. Take the sickle and harvest your crop."
And Olek did as he was told.
Soon all the worthless leaves were cut.

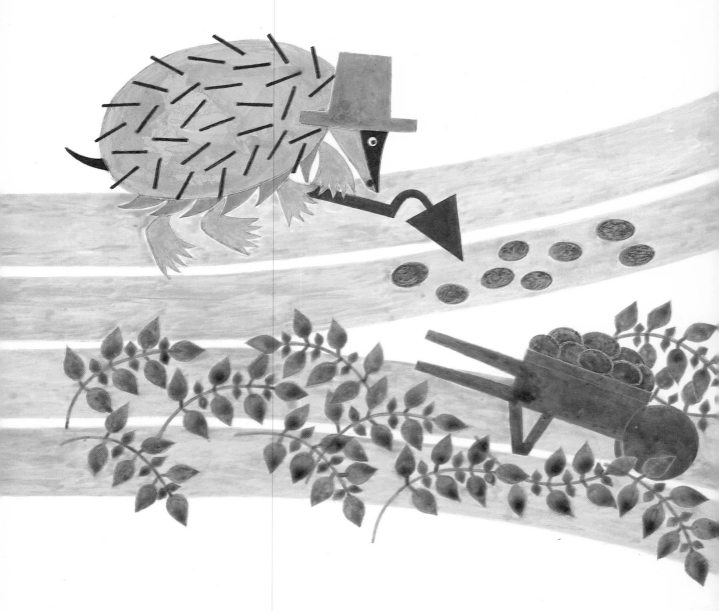

Then it was Hugo's turn. He dug and dug
until he had found all the potatoes.

"Now it is time to pick the apples from your orchard and divide them between us," Hugo said.

So Hugo ended up with
all the potatoes from his
field and half the apples
from Olek's orchard as well.

The next year Hugo and Olek met again. "Would you like to share our crops and fruit again this year?" asked Olek.

"With great pleasure," said Hugo.
"Which half do you want this year—
  the half that grows above the ground
  or the half that grows below?"
"Oh, you will not trick me again!" said Olek.
"I am not so foolish as to take the top half.
  This time I want the half that grows
  below the ground."
"Very well," said Hugo. "We will sow wheat."

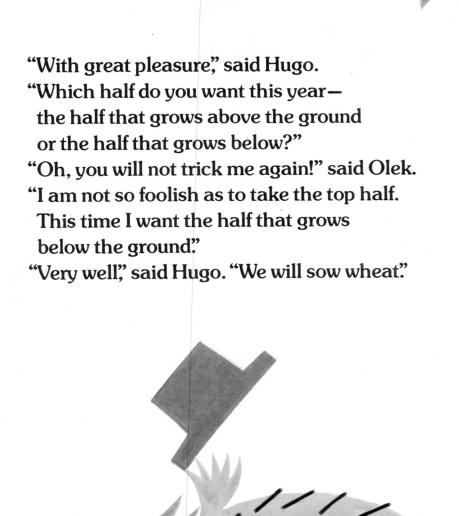

They plowed the field.

They sowed the wheat.

The wheat grew tall and golden.
When harvesttime came, Hugo cut it.

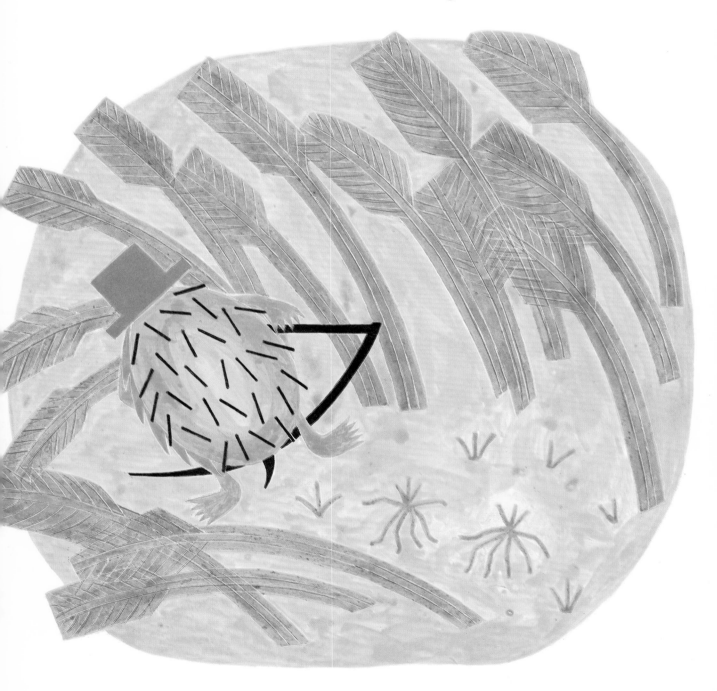

Olek dug up what was left.
But that was only the worthless roots.

"Now we must pick the apples and divide them between us," said Hugo. So this time Hugo had all the wheat from his field and half the apples from Olek's orchard.

Olek saw that he had been tricked again.
He went for help to the judge. The judge
sent for Hugo and said, "Tomorrow
both of you must race to the end
of the wheat field. Whichever
of you wins the race will get all of
the wheat and all of the apples."
Hugo and Olek agreed.

The following day they met at the field.
"Are you ready?" the judge asked. He gave
the signal for the race to start.
Olek was a much faster runner than Hugo,
but no matter how fast the fox ran,
a hedgehog was always in front of him.
And with good reason.

Hugo had several cousins who looked exactly
like him. They were hidden along the field.
When a waiting cousin saw Olek coming,
he started running.
Until the last stretch — Hugo ran that himself.

Olek was only halfway down the field when he heard
the judge shout, "The winner!"
And there stood Hugo at the finish line, scarcely
out of breath. Hugo the hedgehog had once
again outsmarted poor Olek, who had now lost
all of the wheat and all of the apples.

When spring came again,
it was Hugo
who asked Olek
to be his partner.
But Olek refused.